Welcome to The Giggle Club

The Giggle Club is a new series of picture books made to put a giggle into early reading. There are funny stories about a contrary mouse, a dancing fox, a turtle with a trumpet, a pig with a ball, a hungry monster, a laughing lobster, an elephant who sneezes away the jungle, and lots more! Each of these characters is a member of **The Giggle Club**, but anyone can join: just pick up a **Giggle Club** book, read it, and get giggling!

Turn to the checklist on the inside back cover and check off the Giggle Club books you have read.

For Amelia

Copyright © 1995 by Colin West

First U.S. paperback edition 1997

The Library of Congress has cataloged the hardcover edition as follows:

West, Colin.
One day in the jungle / Colin West. — 1st U.S. ed.
Summary: Starting with a butterfly, each successive animal sneezes
louder until the elephant blows away the jungle.
ISBN 1-56402-646-9 (hardcover)
[1. Jungle animals—Fiction.   2. Sneeze—Fiction.]   I. Title
PZ7.W51744On   1995
[E]—dc20   95-7888

ISBN 1-56402-987-5 (paperback)

2 4 6 8 10 9 7 5 3

Printed in Hong Kong

This book was typeset in Plantin.
The pictures were done in watercolor and ink.

Candlewick Press
2067 Massachusetts Avenue
Cambridge, Massachusetts 02140

One Day in the Jungle

COLIN WEST

CANDLEWICK PRESS
CAMBRIDGE, MASSACHUSETTS

One day in the jungle
there was a little sneeze.

"Bless you, Butterfly!" said Lizard.

Next day in the jungle
there was a not-quite-so-little sneeze.

"Bless you, Lizard!"
said Parrot.

Next day in the jungle
there was a medium-sized sneeze.

"Bless you, Parrot!"
said Monkey.

Next day in the jungle
there was a big sneeze.

"Bless you, Monkey!"
said Tiger.

Next day in the jungle
there was a very big sneeze.

"Bless you, Tiger!" said Hippo.

Next day in the jungle
there was an enormous sneeze.

"Bless you, Hippo!"
said Elephant.

Next day in the jungle
there was a **GIGANTIC** sneeze.

"Bless me!" said Elephant.
"I've blown away the jungle!"